Clifford's™ puppy days

GIVING THANKS

by Sarah Fisch

Illustrated by Bob Roper

Based on the Scholastic book series
"Clifford The Big Red Dog"
by Norman Bridwell

No part of this publication may be reproduced in whole or in part, stored in a retrieval system, or transmitted in any form or by any means, electronic, mechanical, photocopying, recording, or otherwise, without written permission of the publisher. For information regarding permission, write to Scholastic Inc., Attention: Permissions Department, 557 Broadway, New York, NY 10012.

ISBN-13: 978-0-545-02842-4

ISBN-10: 0-545-02842-6

Designed by Michael Massen

10 9 8 7 6 5 4 3 2 1   07 08 09 10 11

Printed in the U.S.A.
First printing, October 2007

SCHOLASTIC INC.

| New York | Toronto | London | Auckland | Sydney |
| Mexico City | New Delhi | Hong Kong | Buenos Aires |

With the month of November came a chill in the air.

The last leaves of fall danced in the wind. Clifford loved to chase them.

It was Thanksgiving Day. Mr. and Mrs. Howard started cooking dinner early.

Clifford wanted to be part of the fun.

"Watch out, Clifford!" cried Mrs. Howard.

"Maybe you should go see Emily Elizabeth," said Mr. Howard.

Emily Elizabeth was making decorations.

"Be careful, Clifford!" she said.

"My pictures are still wet!"

I'm in everybody's way today,

Clifford thought sadly.

He walked back to his room.

"What's wrong?" Daffodil asked him.

"I guess today isn't for puppies,"
Clifford answered.

"Thanksgiving is for everyone," said
Daffodil. "Today is the day we give thanks."

"I'm thankful for yummy food and nice naps," Daffodil said. "What are you thankful for, Clifford?"

"Can I be thankful for chew toys?" he asked. "And games of tug-of-war with Jorgé?"

"Sure," Daffodil answered.

"I like sunny days, too," Clifford said.

"And playing ball in the park!"

"That's a good one," Daffodil said.

Clifford felt a lot better.

"I give thanks for Norville, the Sidarskys, and you and Jorgé, too!" he said.

"There is so much to be thankful for!"
Clifford yelped, wagging his tail.

"That's the spirit, Clifford!" Daffodil cheered.

Then Clifford and Daffodil heard a
wonderful sound.

"Time for dinner!" Mrs. Howard called.

At the dinner table, everyone gave thanks.

"I give thanks for this dinner," said Mr.

Howard.

"I give thanks for your decorations!"
Mrs. Howard told Emily Elizabeth.

Emily Elizabeth jumped up from her seat.

She hugged her mom and her dad.

She hugged Clifford and Daffodil, too.

"I give thanks for all of you," she said.

So this is Thanksgiving! thought Clifford.

There were so many reasons to be thankful.

But most of all, Clifford thought, *I give thanks for my family!*

Do You Remember?

Circle the right answer.

1. Which holiday are the Howards celebrating?

   a. Halloween

   b. Thanksgiving

   c. New Year's Day

2. What was Daffodil thankful for?

   a. A cozy home

   b. Jorgé

   c. Yummy food

Which happened first?

Which happened next?

Which happened last?

Write a 1, 2, or 3 in the space after each sentence.

Clifford chased leaves. _____

The family ate Thanksgiving dinner. _____

Clifford felt thankful for ball games in the park. _____

Answers:

Clifford felt thankful for ball games in the park. (2)

The family ate Thanksgiving dinner. (3)

Clifford chased leaves. (1)

2. c

1. b